ZONDERKIDZ

VeggieTown Voyage
Copyright © 2012 by Big Idea, Inc. VEGGIETALES.® character names, likenesses and other indicia are trademarks of Big Idea, Inc. All rights reserved.

Requests for information should be addressed to:
Zonderkidz, 5300 Patterson Ave. SE, Grand Rapids, Michigan 49530

ISBN 978-0-310-72352-3

Lost in Place ISBN 9780310706298 (2005)
Cool Hand Cuke ISBN 9780310707387 (2005)
Ben Hurry ISBN 9780310707431 (2005)

Written by: Cindy Kenney and Doug Peterson
Illustrated by: Michael Moore
Original editor: Cindy Kenney
Original art direction and design: Karen Poth
Cover design: Diane Mielke

Printed in China

12 13 14 15 16 /LPC/ 10 9 8 7 6 5 4 3 2 1

"So do not be afraid. I am with you. Do not be terrified.
I am your God. I will make you strong and help you."

(Isaiah 41:10)

Lost In Place

By Cindy Kenney
Illustrated by Michael Moore

bigidea.com

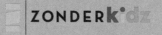

ZONDERVAN.com/
AUTHORTRACKER
follow your favorite authors

"Junior! Come out, come out wherever you are!" Laura called.

"You'll never find me!" Junior Asparagus giggled as he darted down an alley and ran out onto a sidewalk. He dove behind some bushes and snuggled into a hiding spot.

After a few minutes, Junior peeked around the bushes. No sign of Laura. In fact, there was no sign of anything familiar. Where was he?

The sun began to set and darkness crept in. Still no sign of Laura.

Junior slipped out from behind the bushes. He looked to his left, then to his right. He didn't know the way home!

Meanwhile, Back at the Asparagus House...

Laura described to Junior's mom and dad what happened.

"I called and called his name. But he never came out!" she cried.

Junior's mom and dad looked at each other. Where could Junior be?

In the Meantime...

Junior tried to find his way home. He didn't recognize anything or anyone. Turning a corner, he headed down a dark alley. Was it just his imagination, or was something watching him?

As Junior neared the end of the alley, a large, square shadow with heavy footsteps approached.

"*Footsteps*?" Junior mumbled. "In *VeggieTown*?"

Startled by the sound, Junior turned and ran the opposite direction. At the other end of the alley, two large shadows moved toward him. Junior heard heavy breathing. He choked back a tear.

"Junior!" called one of the figures.

How do they know my name? he thought.

"Junior! Where are you?" called the other voice.

It was his mom and dad!

"Boy, am I glad to see you guys! I was really scared!" Junior confessed. "A big monster was chasing after me!"

"Do you mean this nice police officer?" asked Junior's mom.

Junior turned around to see an officer smiling down at him.

"We were worried too, Junior," said his dad. He was out of breath after running all over VeggieTown. "But God watches over you. He's with you wherever you go."

"If you put your trust in God, he will make you strong and help you through anything you're afraid of," added his mom.

Junior was glad to hear that. But he just wanted to go home.

The Next Day...

Junior refused to leave the house. Percy Pea asked him to go to the park. Laura Carrot asked him to ride bikes. His mom and dad encouraged him to go over to a friend's house. But Junior was too afraid to go anywhere.

"Let's go to the Treasure Trove Bookstore," Junior's mom suggested. "You can pick out a good book to read if you're going to stay home all day."

At the Bookstore...

   Mrs. Asparagus told Mr. O'Malley that Junior got lost. She asked him to help them find a good adventure to read.

   "Aye! It just so happens I have a story that takes place in outer space. Let's see...where is it now?" The Irish Potato shuffled through some of the books and said, "Here we go. It's right between the *Using Your Noodle When You Doodle* books and *God Is Bigger Than the Boogie Man*. It's called *Lost in Place*. Take a look at it, lad."

   Inside the storybook Junior saw a spaceship flying through a galaxy filled with stars and planets.

At That Very Moment...

Four words lifted up from the galaxy and swirled around Junior. Four little words tumbling a[nd] twirling through shooting stars: **ONCE UPON A TIME**.

All at Once...

WHOOOOOOOOOOOOOSSSHHHHH! Junior was caught up in the stars
and went

racing,
tumbling,
twirling,

and landed right inside a spaceship.

"The ship's new crew member is here!" Don Quest called out to the Rattleson
family. "Welcome to the Jitterbug 2!"

"Huh?" asked Junior, nervously looking around. Once again, he found himself in unfamiliar territory.

"What happened to the Jitterbug 1?" Junior asked.

"That bug lost its jitter in a meteor storm last year. But I got this ship up and running in no time, and we're back on course. This ship can jitterbug, do the watoosie, and dance a pretty mean Hokey Pokey."

A gourd with squinty eyes turned away from his telescope so he could analyze Junior. "What kind of experience do you have?"

"Umm..." blinked Junior.

"That's Dr. Smirk, our ship's scientist," Mr. Rattleson explained. "But his way of doing things is a little different, if you ask me," he whispered. "The Rattleson family is on their way to find a new home in the Alphabeta Solar System."

"But we can't find our way," Dr. Smirk sneered.

"We keep getting lost," added Mr. Rattleson as he checked several instruments on the Jitterbug 2.

"Lost-is-an-ac-cu-rate-an-swer," beeped a robot. "Dr.-Smirk's-dir-ec-tion-form-u-las-are-in-cor-rect."

"We didn't ask for your opinion, robot," barked Dr. Smirk.

"How do ya do," Pa Rattleson said, changing the subject. "We're the Rattleson family. This here's the rest of the clan—Ma, Penny, Will, and Judy."

"Howdy!" said Ma.

"Kin he help us find our way through this here solar system, Pa?" asked Will.

"Me?" Junior asked, surprised.

Just Then...

The ship began to jitter.

"Hang on, everybody!" called Ma Rattleson.

"How do we do that, Ma?" asked Judy, looking down at her sides.

The ship veered to the left and everyone tipped left. The ship veered to the right, and everyone rolled back to the right. Then the ship bobbled up and down.

"It's a meteor shower!" Don yelled.

Everyone grabbed a shower cap and ran frantically around the ship.

"I'll git some shampoo!"

"I'll git the fresh towels!"

"I'll git an umbrella!"

"Git outta my way, you frazzled, frizzle brain!" Will grumbled.

"You git outta my way, you jittery-jumping bean!" Penny griped in return.

"Stop yer fightin'! We're in a crisis!" yelled Ma Rattleson.

The Jitterbug 2 crew bumped this way and that, causing more problems than helping.

Then came the dreaded words...

"We're off course! We've lost our place in space—again!"

Everyone stopped. They stared at the robot as he confirmed the announcement.

"Oh no!" gulped Junior. He knew his mom and dad wouldn't be able to save him this time!

"Ahhhhhhhhhhhhh!" screamed the Rattlesons.

When Suddenly...

They heard someone yell, "STOP!"

"Umm...er...we probably shouldn't panic," Junior suggested as he took a big gulp of air.

Everyone stopped to stare at Junior. With all eyes focused on him, Junior wondered how he could help the crew of the Jitterbug 2.

"Have you ever thought that we're not alone in all this?" Junior asked.

"Nope," said Will.

"Not me," said Judy.

"Not a chance," agreed Penny.

Junior realized he felt alone, just like the others. Then said to himself,
God watches over you. He is with you wherever you go.

"Hey everybody! God is watching over us, right now," Junior began. "He never leaves us...even when we're in a different solar system!"

Then Junior remembered his mom's words, too.

If you put your trust in God, he will make you strong and help you through anything you're afraid of.

"And God wants us to trust him so he can help us find our way through anything. If we remember that, we can all figure out what to do."

Everyone blinked and looked at each other. Could this be true?

Finally...

Don Quest decided to speak. "I just followed Dr. Smirk's orders!"

"Is that true?" Pa demanded.

Dr. Smirk turned away. "I didn't want to mislead you. But I heard the Alphabeta Solar System only liked Veggies who know their ABC's," he explained. "I don't know mine, so I was afraid no one would like me."

"So you gived us bad directions?" gasped Judy.

"You went and got us lost on purpose?" asked Will.

"Dr. Smirk, you don't have to be afraid either," Junior said. "No matter where you go, you're never alone because God is with you. It doesn't matter if you're lost, or if you find yourself in a new situation. God will help you through anything."

"That-mes-sage-com-putes," agreed the robot. "'Do-not-be-a-fraid. I-am-with-you. Do-not-be-ter-ri-fied. I-am-your-God. I-will-make-you-strong-and-help-you.' Isaiah-41:10."

Don Quest buckled himself back in and turned the ship around, confident that God was watching over them.

Ma and Pa turned back to the controls. "We need some help cleaning the shampoo off these levers!"

"That ain't gonna be a problem, Ma. God kin help us git through anything!" said Will.

"And I can help Dr. Smirk with his ABC's." said Penny.

Dr. Smirk thanked Penny and started to work on a new formula. Knowing God was with him, he trusted he would find a new way to get to the Alphabeta Solar System. So he inserted a new direction formula into the robot.

"Dr.-Smirk's-cal-cu-la-tions-are-cor-rect," confirmed the robot. "We-are-back-on-course."

Everyone cheered.

As the ship headed into the Alphabeta Solar System, several letters swirled into view: **THE END**. Junior waved good-bye as he was pulled back through space.

In a Twinkling...

Junior found himself back inside the Treasure Trove Bookstore.

"*Lost in Place*?" asked Mrs. Asparagus. "Mr. O'Malley, do you have anything else? I don't think Junior wants to read about getting lost."

"That's okay, Mom. I'm never alone because God is with me!" Junior told her.

"Aye, lad! That's true," Mr. O'Malley said with a wink.

Just then, the little bell above the Treasure Trove Bookstore's door began to twinkle. The family that entered looked just like the Rattleson family from the Jitterbug 2!

"Excuse us," said the older grape. "I think we're lost. We sure could use some directions."

"Aye, I'd be happy to help, sir," Mr. O'Malley said. "What are you looking for?"

"Planet Earth."

Junior couldn't hide his surprise.

"Well, then there's no need to fear," Mr. O'Malley answered. "You've already found it!"

"Hands that don't want to work make you poor.
But hands that work hard bring wealth to you."

(Proverbs 10:4)

Cool Hand Cuke

By Cindy Kenney
Illustrated by Michael Moore

bigidea.com

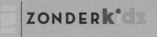

ZONDERVAN.com/
AUTHORTRACKER
follow your favorite authors

"Let's all do the hop, Oh Baby, let's all do the hop."
Jimmy and Jerry sang as they entered the Veggie-HOP café. Junior and Laura were busy working to raise money for the VeggieTown Hospital.

"Junior!" shouted Laura. "Customers!"

Junior rolled his eyes. He dragged himself away from his peanut-butter milk shake and seated Jimmy and Jerry.

Laura took an order at another table.

"Do you have zee French fries?" asked Jean Claude.

"Or zee French toast?" asked Phillipe.

"No," Laura explained. "Everything we serve at the House of Peanut Butter has peanut butter in it."

"Order up!" called the cook.
Laura spotted Junior sitting with Jimmy and Jerry. "Junior! Please get that order!"
"We're not raising much money," Junior moaned.
"C'mon Junior, please!" Laura begged. "It will be worth it, you'll see."

"It's not worth it. I'm wasting my whole summer vacation and I won't have a thing to show for it," Junior grumbled as he jumped out of the booth.

He didn't see Laura, who was carrying a tray full of peanut-butter fritters.

CRASH!

"That's it. I quit," Junior said and stomped out the door.

That evening Junior wandered into the Treasure Trove Bookstore.
"What's got your feathers all ruffled, lad?" Mr. O'Malley asked.
"I don't want to work during summer vacation if I don't get to keep the money," Junior said.

"Looking to get rich, are ya?" the Irish potato said with a wink.

Wham! A big book plopped down in front of Junior.

"A vacation book?" Junior asked.

"Better than that. It's a trip to a farm where you'll find real wealth."

Junior read the title, "Cool Hand Cuke."

As he opened the book, the words "Once Upon A Time" began to swirl around and . . .
WHOOOOOOOOOOOSH!
Junior found himself racing **down**
down
down
right into the middle of a farm.

"Ah! The new farmhand," a tomato said.

"I'm Hot Hand Tomato," he said. "This is my partner, Cool Hand Cuke."

He shoved a basket at Junior and said, "We've got lots of work to do before sundown. You can help us finish up in the barn."

"This is supposed to be my vacation," whined Junior.

In the barn they were greeted by a grape with mirrored sunglasses.

"If you fill your baskets before sundown, you get a prize from the box," barked the grape. "If you feed the chickens by ten, you get a prize from the box. Sweep the barn by noon, and you get a prize from the box."

Junior glanced at the prize box. It contained lots of stuff like a yo-yo,
tennis shoes, and a sombrero, but not riches.

"Finishin' up over here, boss," said Cool Hand Cuke. He showed him a full basket of eggs.

"Pick your prize out of the box, Cuke," said the boss.

Cool Hand Cuke eyed a big, colorful sombrero. "Oooh, I'm going to wear this into town! Junior, Hot Hand, would you come too?"

"Thanks!" Junior said. "That's better than collecting a bunch of eggs and sweeping a dirty old barn!"

When they got to town, Cool Hand Cuke and the tomato hung a sign over a booth. It read: Eggs for Sale.

"Oh, I get it," Junior said. "This is how we get rich! We sell the eggs so we can go on vacation. Good idea."

The eggs sold like crazy. Their job complete, Junior, Cool Hand Cuke, and Hot Hand Tomato headed toward the city hospital.

Doctors, nurses, and patients filled the room. "What's going on?" asked
Junior.

"Time for a square dance!" Cool Hand shouted.

"There are only three of us," Hot Hand whispered. "We can't make a
square. How about a triangle?"

"Excellent idea!" agreed Cool Hand. Two gourds called out commands as Cuke, Hot Hand, and Junior began to do-si-do.

"Isosceles!"

"Right angle!"

"Look how happy we're making the patients," whispered Hot Hand.

When the music stopped, Hot Hand called for a break. "I'll make the tamales!"

"I'll get the drinks," Cuke offered. He headed toward the watercooler. "Sure wish we had something special to give them besides tamales."

"Do you have any peanut butter?" Junior asked.
Junior whipped up some peanut-butter shakes and served the patients.
Cool Hand Cuke got ready for his juggling act.

"Everybody loves this," the tomato whispered.
"Juggle thirty eggs today, Cuke!" yelled a pea.
"Forty!" chimed in another.
"Fifty!" called the gourds.
"Nobody can juggle fifty eggs!" shouted a nurse.

"I can!" boasted the cucumber. "That's why they call me Cool Hand Cuke."
Everyone cheered as Cool Hand Cuke began to juggle. Ten . . . twenty . . .
thirty . . . forty . . . and then fifty eggs!

After the party, Cuke removed his sombrero. It was filled with the money from the eggs they'd sold.

Junior's eyes popped open. "We're rich!"

"This money is for the hospital," said Cuke.
"But weren't we working to get rich?"
"What we have here is a failure to appreciate," said the tomato.
"What does that mean?" asked Junior.

"Junior, we are rich. Look at that little carrot over there. See the smile on her face? And the pea over there? See how happy he is to have a new wheelchair? We are rich in friendship and love," Cuke said.

Hot Hand showed Junior a card the patients had made. It said two simple words: THANK YOU!

"God says, 'Hands that don't want to work make you poor. But hands that work hard bring wealth to you,'" the tomato explained.

"I've got a whole summer ahead of me! Just think what I can do for others!" Junior smiled.

Just then two words floated out of the speakers: **THE END**.
Junior was swept up into the spinning letters.

After Junior landed back in the bookstore he rushed over to the café.
"I'm really sorry," Junior told Laura. "I'll help you raise money for the
VeggieTown Hospital. Maybe we could even provide entertainment."

"Really?" Laura asked.

"You bet! After all, hands that don't want to work make you poor. But hands that work hard bring wealth to you."

Junior began clearing the tables. Laura smiled at her friend. "What kind of entertainment did you have in mind?"

"Do you know how to juggle eggs?"

"We hope for what we don't have yet.
So we are patient as we wait for it."

(Romans 8:25)

Ben Hurry

By Doug Peterson
Illustrated by Michael Moore

bigidea.com

"Are we there yet?" asked Junior and Laura.
One minute later, they asked again, "Are we there yet?"
Thirty seconds later . . .
"ARE WE—"

"No, we're not there yet," grumbled Bob the Tomato.

"Kids, you'll be much happier if you learn to wait," added Mr. Asparagus. "Waiting means being patient. And patience is a gift from God."

But Junior and Laura didn't think they could wait another millisecond to get to the new Lobster-Land Theme Park. They felt like they were going to explode.

Suddenly, Bob stopped the car.

"Traffic," he growled. "Everyone in VeggieTown must be going to Lobster-Land today."

He was right. Cars on the road stretched for miles. It was going to take forever to get there. Even Dad Asparagus was getting impatient.

BUDS
HORSE FARM

"That's it! I'm not waiting another second!" Bob said. He turned quickly onto a side road. "I know a shortcut."

Junior and Laura cheered as their car began to move again. But the shortcut led them onto a bumpy, narrow road. Even worse, they got stuck behind a slow truck carrying a load to the Nails 'R' Us hardware store.

"Are we there yet?" asked Junior and Laura.

Thump!
The truck in front of them hit a big bump, spilling nails all over the road.

"Look out!"

Pop! Pow!
Sssssss. Their front tires were flatter than squished pancakes.

The next day Junior and Laura went to the Treasure Trove Bookstore. "I can't believe we didn't make it to Lobster-Land," Junior said.

"We'll have to wait forever to go again," muttered Laura.

"Wait right here," said Mr. O'Malley, the owner of the store. "I've got the perfect book for you."

The old potato shuffled to the bookshelf like a tired turtle. "I think the book is in the 'Where's the Fire?' section. Here it is, right next to the edible cookbooks."

Junior and Laura opened the book to a picture of a huge Roman ship. Soldiers in gleaming armor stood on the deck.

As they looked at the page, four giant words floated up from the book. Four simple words: Once Upon A Time.

The words swirled around Junior and Laura. They whirled and twirled and . . .

WHOOOOOOOOOOOSH!

Junior and Laura tumbled **down**
down
down.

Whomp!

Junior and Laura landed on the deck of the ship they had seen in the book. A second later they were being pushed along by a little Roman pea named Ben Hurry. "Hurry up, hurry up! We don't have all day. Get rowing!"

"Move, move, move!" yelled another pea named Maximus Hurrius, or Max, for short. "We've got to get to Rome now!"

"What's going on?" Junior asked as the peas dragged him and Laura below deck.

"No time to talk!" barked Ben Hurry.

Below deck were rows and rows of Veggies, pulling on huge wooden oars.

"We're missing two rowers!" exclaimed Ben. "Take a seat! Hurry!"

"There's not a moment to lose," added Max as he pushed Laura onto a bench.

"What's the rush?" Laura snapped.
"We're going to Rome to see the Monster Chariot Show!" shouted Ben.
"Wait until you see those monster chariots drive over rows of little chariots!"
yelled Max. "It's the coolest thing. But we gotta get there as fast as possible!"

Junior and Laura rowed like crazy.

A Roman cucumber sat in front of the rowers and beat on a drum. The faster the drum beat, the faster everyone had to row.

"Are we there yet?" asked Ben Hurry.

"No! Increase to Impatient Speed!" yelled Max.

"Impatient Speed!" repeated the drummer, and he began to drum even faster.

The rowers picked up speed.

"Are we there yet?" asked Ben.

"No!" shouted Max. "Increase to Freaky-Fast Speed!"

"Freaky-Fast Speed!" repeated the drummer. Then the cucumber began to drum so fast that sparks flew. The rowers rowed so fast that some of the oars snapped.

"This is crazy!" Junior gasped, trying to keep up.

But Ben didn't care. He started to sing: "Row, row, row the boat, quickly down the stream! Hurry, hurry, hurry, hurry! Or I'm going to scream!"
"Faster!" yelled Max. "It's taking us forever to get to Rome!"

Up ahead, Junior spotted hundreds of ships headed toward Rome.
"It's a traffic jam. We've got to slow down!" shouted Junior.
"No way!" boomed Ben. "Increase to Warped Speed!"
"Warped Speed!" yelled the cucumber. He drummed faster than the speed of light.
"We can't keep up!" Laura gasped.
Their ship zipped across the water, headed straight for the long line of boats.

"We're going to ram another ship!" shouted one of the rowers.
"We've got to stop!"
"Nothing doing!" yelled Max.
"Move into the passing lane!" Ben ordered. "Hurry! Hurry! Hurry!"
But it was too late. They rammed into another ship.

Cra-a-ack!

Wood splintered. Water gushed in through a hole in the front of their boat.

"Keep rowing!" cried Ben.

"Hurry!"

Water came up to the drummer's nose. "Are we there yet?" he gurgled.

Within minutes, the ship sank. Some of the ship's crew swam to shore. Everyone else climbed onto floating chunks of wood. Junior and Laura wound up on the same piece of wood as Max, Ben, and the drummer.

"You really need to learn how to wait," Junior told Ben. "I should know. I have a hard time waiting for things too. But patience is a gift from God."

"It would have made me so happy to get to Rome as fast as I could," said Ben.

"When you can't wait, you usually end up unhappy," said Laura.

The drummer hit his soggy drum. "I'm definitely unhappy," he muttered.

Later that day, Junior, Laura, the drummer, and the two peas finally reached Rome. But they missed the Monster Chariot Show.

"We can still make the Brutus 500 chariot race," said the drummer.

"We'll have to hurry," said Max.

"No need to hurry," Ben said. "Patience is a gift from God, you know."

They missed the beginning of the chariot race, but they still had a great time. When the race was over, two large words appeared on the side of the winning chariot: **THE END**.

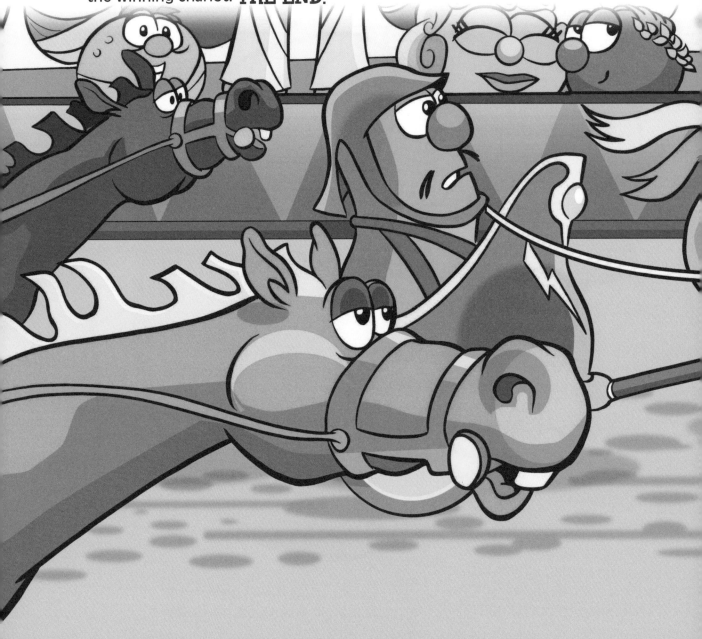

"It's time for us to leave," said Junior sadly.
"So soon?" said Ben.
"Will you come back and visit?" asked Max.
"Maybe some day," said Laura.
"We'll be waiting."

In a flash, Junior and Laura found themselves back in the Treasure Trove Bookstore.

"Welcome home!" shouted Mr. O'Malley. "I want to hear all about your adventure. But first, you might like to see these. I've got tickets to Lobster-Land, and I'm taking both of you!" he announced.

Junior and Laura couldn't believe their ears. "When are we going? When? When? When?!"

"Well, that's the catch," said Mr. O'Malley. "We can't go for two weeks."

The smiles suddenly vanished from Junior's and Laura's faces. "Oh."

But ever so slowly, the grins returned.

"We can wait!" Laura declared.

"That's the spirit!" said Mr. O'Malley. "After all, Rome wasn't built in a day. It took patience."

"Lobster-Land, here we come!" said Junior.

Were they there yet?

No, they weren't. But that was okay. They were happy to wait.